Leapfrog World Tales

Little Tiger
and the
Fire

by Julia Jarman

Illustrated by Roberta Angaramo

W
FRANKLIN WATTS
LONDON • SYDNEY

First published in 2010 by
Franklin Watts
338 Euston Road
London
NW1 3BH

Franklin Watts Australia
Level 17/207 Kent Street
Sydney
NSW 2000

A CIP catalogue record for this book is available
from the British Library.

ISBN 978 0 7496 9418 0 (hbk)
ISBN 978 0 7496 9424 1 (pbk)

Series Editor: Jackie Hamley
Editor: Melanie Palmer
Series Advisor: Catherine Glavina
Series Designer: Peter Scoulding

Printed in China

Franklin Watts is a division of
Hachette Children's Books,
an Hachette UK company.
www.hachette.co.uk

This tale comes from India. Can you point to India on a map?

Long ago, Uncle Tiger loved to cook and Little Tiger loved his cooking.

But one day the cooking
fire went out.

Uncle Tiger hurried to the village to get some wood.

When the villagers saw the tiger, they all ran away.

"I only want some wood
for my fire," Tiger pleaded.

Uncle Tiger went home without any wood – but he had a good idea.

"Little Tiger, the villagers are scared of me. You must go to get the wood. And hurry, I'm hungry!"

So Little Tiger set off ...

... but he stopped to play
with some monkeys.

When he did reach the
village, he forgot what
he'd come for.

15

"A bowl of milk?" said one villager.

"A fresh fish?" asked another.

"Somewhere soft to sleep?" another guessed.

"Purr-haps," purred
Little Tiger.

19

Meanwhile, Uncle Tiger
was getting hungrier.

Where was Little Tiger?

He went to look for him.

Uncle Tiger prowled through the village until he found Little Tiger, fast asleep!

"LITTLE TIGER," he roared. "You are NOT a tiger, you are a CAT!"

"Purr-haps," yawned
Little Tiger.

So Uncle Tiger went home
and ate his dinner raw.

Soon all the tigers got used to eating raw meat.

And cats got used to living with people, and enjoying their cooking!

Puzzle 1

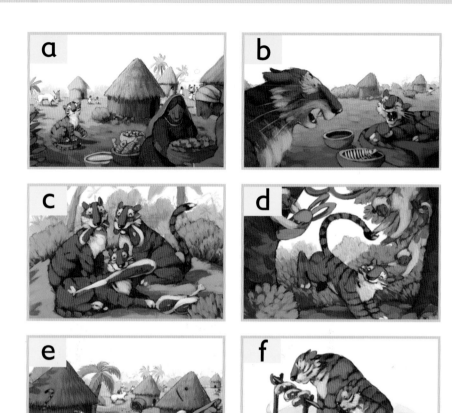

Put these pictures in the correct order.
Now tell the story in your own words.
What different endings can you think of?

Puzzle 2

forgetful   scary

sleepy

worried   fierce

curious

terrified   brave

scared

Choose the correct words for the characters. Which words are incorrect? Turn over to find the answers.

Answers

Puzzle 1

The correct order is: 1f, 2e, 3d, 4a, 5b, 6c

Puzzle 2

Little Tiger: the correct words are forgetful, sleepy

The incorrect word is scary

Uncle Tiger: the correct words are curious, worried

The incorrect word is fierce

Villagers: the correct words are scared, terrified

The incorrect word is brave

Look out for Leapfrog World Tales:

Chief Five Heads
ISBN 978 0 7496 8593 5*
ISBN 978 0 7496 8599 7

Baba Yaga
ISBN 978 0 7496 8594 2*
ISBN 978 0 7496 8600 0

Issun Boshi
ISBN 978 0 7496 8595 9*
ISBN 978 0 7496 8601 7

The Frog Emperor
ISBN 978 0 7496 8596 6*
ISBN 978 0 7496 8602 4

The Gold-Giving Snake
ISBN 978 0 7496 8597 3*
ISBN 978 0 7496 8603 1

The Bone Giant
ISBN 978 0 7496 8598 0*
ISBN 978 0 7496 8604 8

Bluebird and Coyote
ISBN 978 0 7496 9415 9*
ISBN 978 0 7496 9421 0

Anansi the Banana Thief
ISBN 978 0 7496 9416 6*
ISBN 978 0 7496 9422 7

Brer Rabbit and the Well
ISBN 978 0 7496 9417 3*
ISBN 978 0 7496 9423 4

Little Tiger and the Fire
ISBN 978 0 7496 9418 0*
ISBN 978 0 7496 9424 1

No Turtle Stew Today
ISBN 978 0 7496 9419 7*
ISBN 978 0 7496 9425 8

Too Many Webs for Anansi
ISBN 978 0 7496 9420 3*
ISBN 978 0 7496 9426 5

*hardback